Curious George®
VISITS A POLICE STATION

Adapted from the Curious George film series

edited by Margret Rey and Alan J. Shalleck

1 9 8 7

Houghton Mifflin Company, Boston

Library of Congress Cataloging-in-Publication Data

Curious George visits a police station.

"Adapted from the Curious George film series."
Summary: Curious George creates havoc at the
new police station when he accidentally locks the
mayor and the police chief in one of the cells.
[1. Monkeys—Fiction.   2. Police stations—
Fiction]   I. Rey, Margret.   II. Shalleck, Alan J.
III. Curious George visits a police station (Motion
picture)
PZ7.C92187   1987   [E]   87-3561
ISBN 0-395-45349-6

Copyright © 1987 by Houghton Mifflin Company and Curgeo Agencies, Inc.

Printed in the United States of America.

Y 10 9 8 7 6 5 4 3 2 1

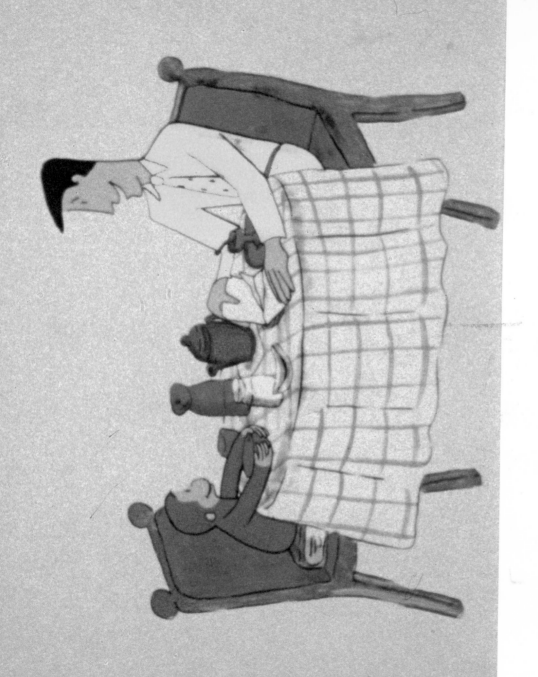

"We've been invited to the new police station, George," said his friend.

The police chief, the mayor, and other guests were standing on the steps when they arrived.

The first thing they saw inside
was the new alarm system.

George was curious.
He wanted to get a closer look.

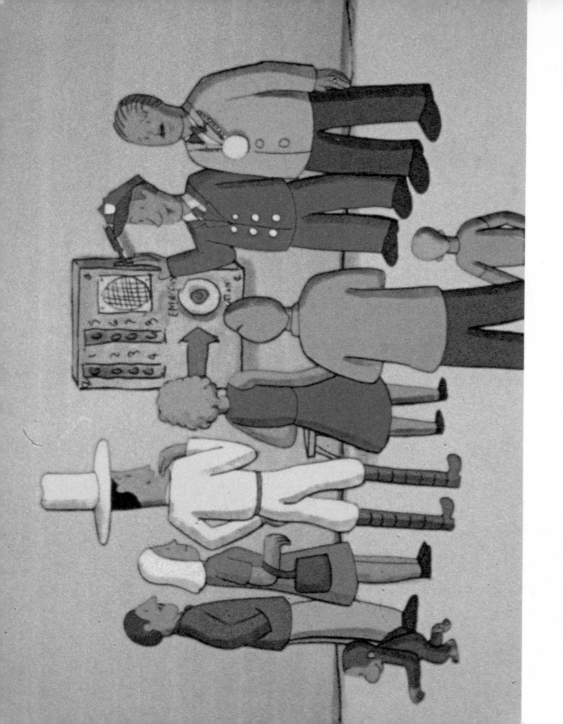

But it was too crowded, so he wandered off to find something else to look at.

In the basement, he found rows of jail cells.
Now George could have some fun.

He climbed up the bars
and swung from cell to cell.

While George was busy clanging doors,
the mayor and the chief came down
to inspect the cells. George did not see them.

Clang! George had locked them up.

"Help!" the mayor shouted.
"Who did that?"

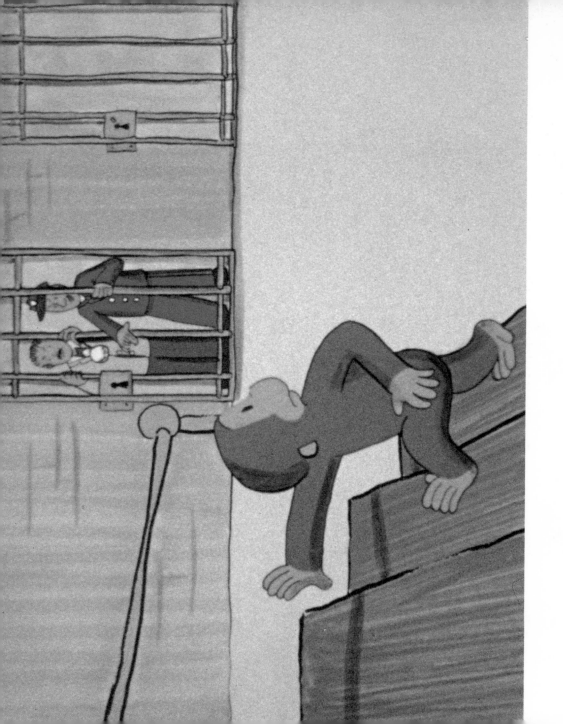

"It was that little monkey!" the chief cried.
"GUARDS! GET HIM!"
But no one heard, and George ran away.

George ran by the alarm system, then he stopped.
Now he could get a closer look.

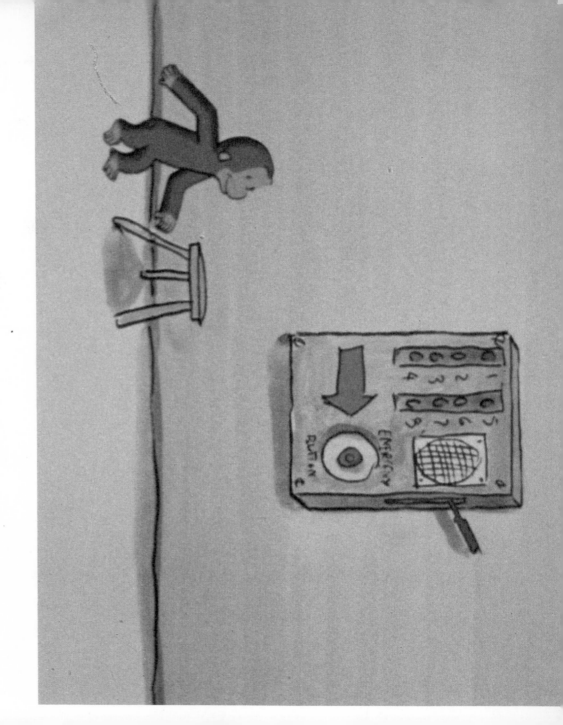

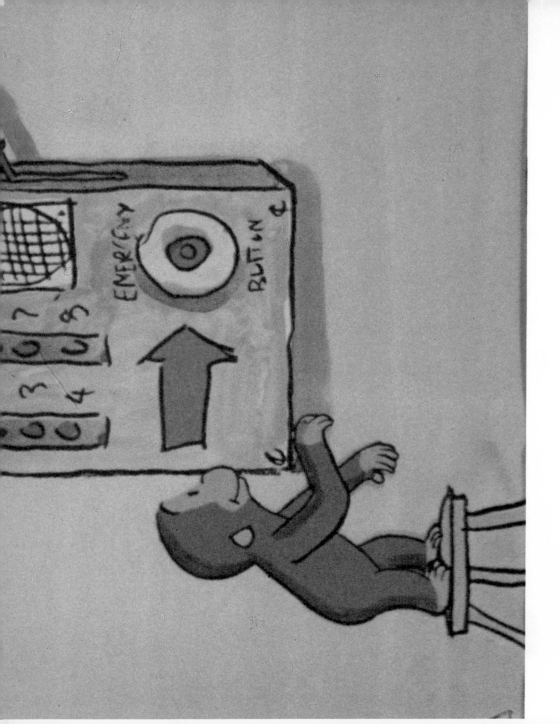

George was curious.

What would happen if he pushed that red button?

George had to find out, so he pushed it.

Suddenly, sirens were screaming!

Policemen came running from every direction.

Now George was really in trouble.
He ran down to the basement.
A policeman ran after him.

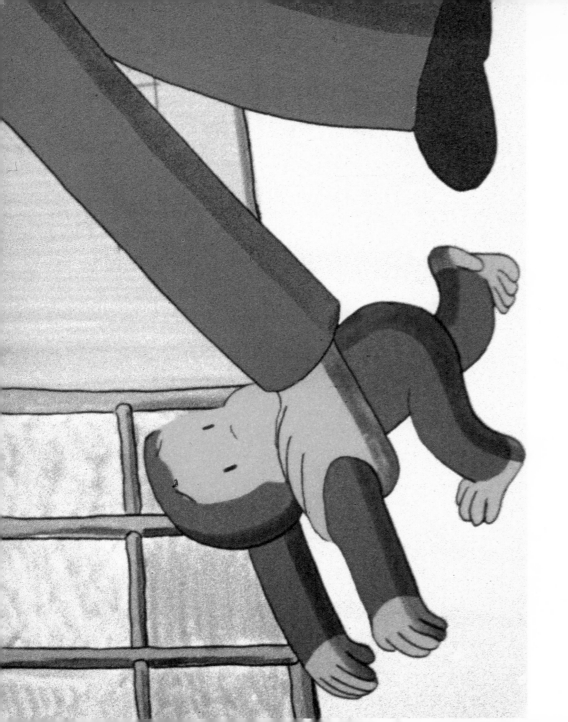

George was caught.

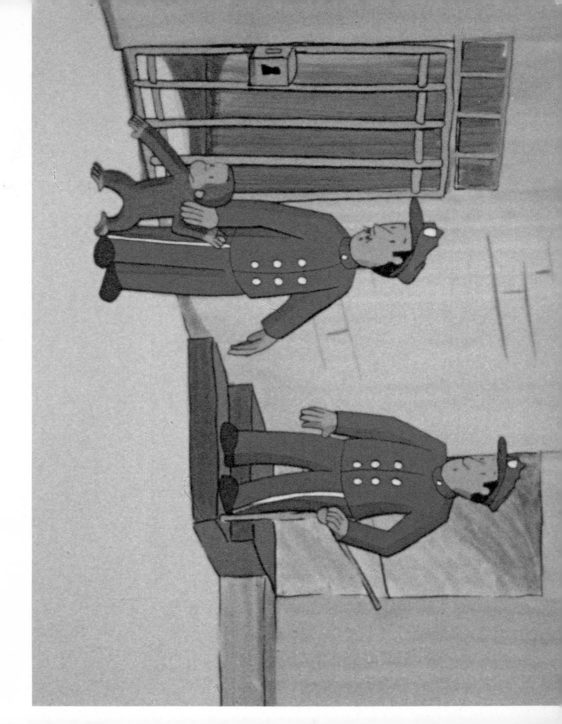

"Lock him up!" they heard someone cry.
It was the mayor and the chief!

"Will someone please get us out of here?" the chief shouted.

The policeman holding George asked,
"Should I lock him up?"

"Well," the chief said, "he did lock us up, but then he also led you fellows down here to get us out. I guess we'll let him go."

"Now let's go upstairs and get on with the ceremony," said the mayor.

George was left alone in the basement, and he was soon busy swinging from cell to cell once more.

In the middle of the ceremony, a policeman came and whispered in the chief's ear. "We have a problem. One of the jail cells got locked again."

"Not again! Where's that monkey?"

They rushed down to see
who got locked up this time.
Were they surprised when they found out.

It was George.

"I hope you learned your lesson,"
said the chief. "I'll give you
one more chance."

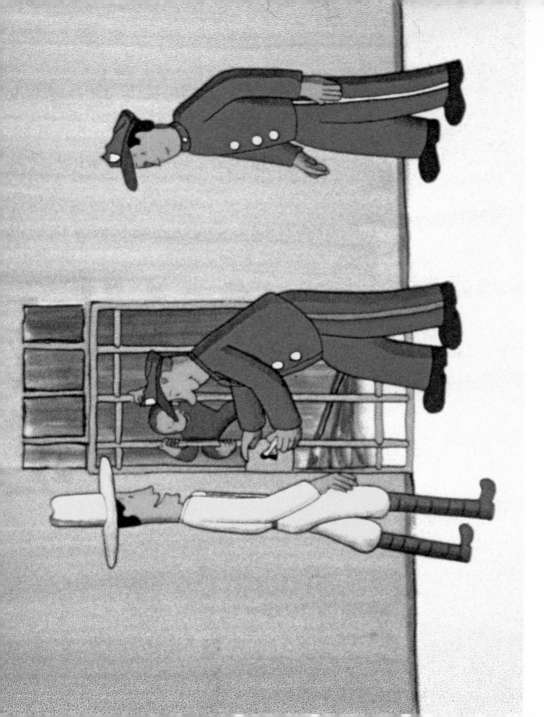

"Thanks, Chief!" said the man with the yellow hat.
He had been looking for George everywhere.

The chief opened the door and George jumped into his friend's arms. "Let's go home," said the man. And that's what they did.